Praise for

THE HALF-GOD OF RAINFALL

'Part Homeric-style epic, part female-focused revenge
tragedy, *The Half-God of Rainfall* stretches the boundaries of
poetry and prose in the way that only Inua Ellams can. Each
line feels as though it's carved into stone – solid, striking,
glinting with beauty, but steeped in hard-edged truth.
The Half-God of Rainfall is a true story for the ages,
as well as for the politics of the present day'

BRIDGET MINAMORE

'For twenty-first-century readers who have fallen into the
rhythm of the courts, this is mythopoetics at its best. By
the strength of its careful braiding of song and swift slashes
through a cross-pantheon of Yoruba and Greek deities,
The Half-God of Rainfall stitches us into a single breath of
wonder and shared delight at the journey of OluDemi
Modupe. Inua Ellams possesses an intuitive and fluid
grasp of the eternal virtues and heroic narratives that
constitute our transglobal imaginations'

MAJOR JACKSON

THE HALF-GOD OF RAINFALL

Inua Ellams

4th ESTATE • *London*

4th Estate
An imprint of HarperCollins*Publishers*
1 London Bridge Street
London SE1 9GF

www.4thEstate.co.uk

First published in Great Britain in 2019 by 4th Estate

1

A catalogue record for this book is
available from the British Library

ISBN 978-0-00-832477-3

Printed and bound in Great Britain by
CPI Group (UK) Ltd, Croydon, CR0 4YY

MIX
Paper from
responsible sources
FSC **FSC® C007454**
www.fsc.org

This book is produced from independently certified FSC paper
to ensure responsible forest management.

For more information visit: www.harpercollins.co.uk/green

For Veronica Ellams, Mariam Asuquo,
Hadiza Alex Ellams, Claire Trévien,
Annabel Stapleton Crittendon, Imogen Butler Cole,
Joelle Taylor and Michaela Coel.

In solidarity with women who have spoken against or
stood up to male abuses of power in all its forms.

I'm a poet so I can empathise with minor gods
                                                — *Chuma Nwokolo*

The first madness was that we were born,
that they stuffed a god into a bag of skin
                                                — *Akwaeke Emezi*

I, too, once dribbled that old bubble, happiness,
and found in time the scramble and the rules
            doubtful
                                                — *W Belvin*

I'm a black ocean, leaping and wide,
welling and swelling I bear in the tide
                                                — *Maya Angelou*

Portrait of Prometheus
as a basketball player.

His layup will start from mountains
not with landslide, rumble or gorgon clash
of titans, but as shadow-fall across stream –
some thief-in-the-night-black-Christ-
type stealth. In the nights before this,
his name, whispered in small circles, muttered
by demigods and goddesses, spread rebellious,
rough on the tongues of whores and queens,
pillows pressed between thighs, moaning.
Men will call him father, son or king
of the court. His stride will ripple oceans,
feet whip-crack quick, his back will scar,
hunched over, a silent storm about him.
Both hands scorched and bleeding;
You see nothing but sparks splash off
his palms, nothing but breeze beneath
his shuck 'n' jive towards the basket
carved of darkness, net of soil and stars.
Fearing nothing of passing from legend to myth
he fakes left, crossover, dribbles down
the line and then soars – an eagle chained
to hang time.

                              – *Inua Ellams*

ACT

ONE

BOOK I

Òrúnmilà, the God of vision and fiction,
whose unique knowing is borderless, whose wisdom
unmatched, who witnessed the light of all creation,

to whom all stories are lines etched deep in his palms,
from the heavens above Nigeria read the qualm
of oncoming conflict, shook his head and looked down.

- x -

The local boys had chosen grounds not too far from
the river, so a cooled breeze could blow them twisting
in the heat. The boys had picked clean its battered palms,

leaves left from previous years, to make this their grounding,
their patch, their pitch. These local lads levelled it flat,
stood two shortened telephone poles up, centering

both ends of the field. Then they mounted tyres, strapped
one atop each pole and stitched strips of fishing nets
to these black rims. Court lines were drawn in charcoal mashed

into a paste and the soil held the dark pigment,
the free throw lines' glistening geometry perfect.
They called it Battle Field, The Court of Kings, The Test,

for this was where warriors were primed from the rest,
where generals were honoured and mere soldiers crushed.
Basketball was more than sport, the boys were obsessed.

They played with a righteous thirst. There were parries, thrusts,
shields and shots, strategies and tactics, land won and
lost, duels fought, ball like a missile, targets | + | locked, such

that Ògún, the Òrìṣà God of War, would stand
and watch. He'd stand and watch. The Gods were watching on.
One child, named Demi, was kept from play. He was banned.

He'd crouch on the edge of the court watching boys turn
and glide in the reach towards the rim, a chasm,
a cavernous emptiness between him and them.

He was banned from games for if they lost, tears would come.
Demi would drench his shirt, soak his classroom and flood
whole schools as once he'd done their pitch, the soil swollen,

poles sunk, it all turned to swamp for weeks. Their lifeblood,
the balletic within them, their game had been stalled.
They never forgave him turning their world to mud.

They resented more than they feared Demi and called
him 'Town Crier', loud, mercilessly chanting this
as they crossed over the brown orb, dribbling, they'd call

Town Crier! Watch this! They worshipped Michael Jordan, ripped
his moves from old games. They'd practise trash-talking, those
dark boys, skin singing to the heat. They'd try to fit

Nigerian tongues round American accents – close
but not close enough – *Dat all you ghot mehn? Ghottu
du betta mehn, youh mama so fat, giant clothes*

no fit cover her hass! till a fist-fight broke through
their game and war spilled out, the Gods laughing, the ball
r o l l i n g towards Demi . . . who, that day, bent to scoop

it up, desperate to join their lush quarrel and all
he asked for was one shot, the five foot four of him
quivering on the court. *No* said Bolu, stood tall,

the King of the court *You'll miss and cry. Boys, grab him!*
Demi fought in their grip, eyes starting to water,
Just one shot or I'll cry and drown this pitch he screamed,

his voice slicing the sky, clouds gathering over.
You small boy! You no get shame? Remember this belt?
Pass the ball before I whip you even harder!

But the King's voice hushed as the earth began to melt,
the soil dampen, telephone poles tilt and great tears
pool in Demi's wild eyes. Far off, Modupe felt

that earth wane. Modupe, Demi's mother, her fears
honed by her child, knowing what danger wild water
could do let loose on land, left everything – her ears

seeking Demi's distinct sobbing – the market where
she worked, utter chaos in her wake, in her vaults
over tables stacked with fruits and fried goods, the air

parting   for her, the men unable to find fault
in the thick-limbed smooth movement that was her full form.
Back at the court, Demi held on as the boys waltzed

around his pinned-down form beneath the threatening storm
One shot oh! Just one! the arena turning mulch
beneath them. Alarmed, the King yelled *Fine! But shoot from*

where you lay. Demi spat the soil out his mouth, hunched
till he could see one dark rim, gathered his sob back
into him and let fly the ball, his face down, crunched.

Years later Bolu would recount that shot. Its arch.
Its definite flight path, the slow rise, peak and wane
of its fall through the fishing net. Swish. Its wet thwack

on damp earth, the skies clearing, then silence. *Again*
Bolu said, pushing the ball to his chest. *Again.*
Demi, do it again. And the crowds went insane.

The rabble grew and swirled around them on the plain
of damp soil chanting *Again!* each time Demi drained
the ball down the net. Modupe arrived and craned

her neck but couldn't glimpse Demi, so, a fountain
of worry, she splashed at one. *What happened? Tell me!*
You didn't see? Town Crier can't miss! He just became

the Rainman! Make it rain, baby! Yes! Shoot that three!
Ten more shots, each flawless, and they hoisted Demi
onto their shoulders, his face a map of pure glee.

Two things Modupe would never forget – that glee
when Demi became the Rainman was the second.
The first, the much darker: how Demi was conceived.

BOOK II

They say when Modupe was born her own mother,
who worshipped the God of vision and fiction, screamed
when she foresaw the future looks of her daughter:

the iridescent moon she'd resemble, the dream
she'd seem to men and thus the object she'd become.
Her mother had known these men her whole life, had seen

them all ... from the weak and pathetic overcome
by lust, to warlords who to crush rebellion
would attack the women to daunt their men and sons.

She'd suffered such brands of violence. It had churned
her for years. Knowing her child would need protection
from a God who could *wash* the eyes of men and numb

their hot senses, the young mother took swift action,
stole her child to the shrine of the River Goddess
Osún, she prayed for protection, poured libation,

straddled her daughter and to show conviction lest
Osún think this a token act, split her own womb
with a knife, the blood pooling on her daughter's chest.

Skies above Nigeria, far above the gloom,
in the heavens over Earth where the Òrìṣà,
the Yoruba Gods and Goddesses lived and loomed

Osún wailed. Voice like cyclones, she swore an oath as
Modupe's mother bled: no mortal man would know
this child. *No one will come near!* She swore to the stars,

to the galaxy's dark. Osún's oath shook black holes.
Woe to those who would test me! To those who would try!
She made Modupe her high priestess, her go-to,

her vessel, her *self* on Earth, and built her a shrine
and compound by the river's edge, where the soil soaked
with water meant Modupe could move land, unwind

the swamp into a weapon should she be provoked.
And though it became widely known that Modupe
was untouchable, it never stopped men. It stoked

their prying eyes and their naked hunger. On clear
nights they'd secretly watch her. They'd see the full moon
beaming to the rippling and pristine waters where

she bathed. The water, like liquid diamonds, cocooned
her with light. This happened years later, when she was
fully grown and legends of her beauty had bloomed

into foolish shameless lustful moans and prayers
pitched to Sàngó, the brash God of Thunder, who too
would grab his godhood, gaze at Modupe and pause

to stroke himself. If she could humble thunder too
how safe was she among men? In his palace up
among storm clouds, Sàngó squeezed himself, slow, imbued

with dreams of her beneath him, dark skin ripe, breast cupped
when   BOOM!   rang the doors of his palace, the room shook
BOOM!   *I'M THE GOD OF THUNDER! WHO DARES INTERRUPT...*

Oh, greetings, Osún. She swept in. Her garments took
the deep thick greenish tinge of low waves. Her crown quaked
with new-moon jewels. The River Goddess, angry, shook.

Sàngó! That's Modupe! You shouldn't even take
a peek! You know the oath I took   /   Yes but   /   Nothing!
Now, go clean yourself. I bring news. For your own sake.

Moments later Sàngó returned, low-thundering
with each step. *Don't sulk! A ah! Now, I know his name
angers you, but the Greek God-King, Zeus, is warring*

*and mankind again is at risk. Modupe's name
is drawn among the list of likely casualties
if you react, Sàngó. Now, our sage who has tamed*

*all possibilities, Òrúnmilà, who sees
all stories, him, our God of vision and fiction
who saw the light of all creation, sends his pleas.*

*Tonight, he says: Sàngó, be still. Cause no friction.
Whatever happens, throw no thunder, hold your bolts,
for an omen rules the skies. Be wise. Use caution.*

And just as Osún spoke, then struck a lightning bolt.
A ferocious white blaze shook the grand hall and struck
its ancient paintings to confetti, jolting volts

of fire burned the cracked pillars. *Look how he mocks
us! Thrice now my dear! No!* Sàngó grabbed his loudest
thunder, his blackest fire, his closest friend, ducked

before Osún could utter any calming words
and was gone! Osún stared from the broken stairs down
to Earth, down at young Modupe, and feared the worst.

BOOK III

For thousands of years, Gods enjoyed full dominion
over the lives of men. From the northernmost poles
to the southern, from the east of the sun's rise down

to the west of the sun's set, men promised their souls
and gave their all in penitent servitude but
this century marked a change. Their lives, from sole

god-worship, turned to fleshy pleasures and the glut
of property. As prayers which fed and assuaged
the might of Gods dwindled, they felt their power cut.

Zeus, who had been glorified on film, song and stage,
felt this keenly, grew vengeful and sharpened his bolts.
That lightning lord, that God-father, whose ancient rage

once frightened kings, whose influence, whose merest hopes
were turned to laws, and laws supreme, realised too
late this dwindling servitude of men and hurled volts.

He killed them. Other Gods grew benevolent, cooled
down, conserving power, but Zeus smote those who strayed
from him, bolts asunder, this way, that, so thrice through

Sàngó's wide window Zeus' terrible aim flayed
the walls and Sàngó had enough, thundered, vexed,
sped towards Mount Olympus. As he charged, his way

was watched by other thunder-gods: from Egypt – Set,
Chaac – Mayan, Indra – Hindu, from China – Feng Lung,
Whaitiri – Māori, Thor – Norse God and the rest

too numerous to count watched Sàngó's raging run
to Olympus knowing chaos would come. Sàngó's
first bolt hit the doors with such force Hera's throne spun.

Hera – Queen of the Greek Gods, screamed to Apollo
– God of Archery to take arms against Sàngó,
as Ares – God of War, sat back to watch the show.

Artemis – Goddess of Hunting, grasped her long bow
but Sàngó burned it to ashes, his black fire
wild in his hands. He hurled it at Hera, grasped low

its shaft when it struck her throne, whipped back its fire
at Apollo. With the two archers down he hewed
from a distance. He struck column after spire

after pillar after stone. Sàngó's anger stood
down every attack, slaying their weapons until
Zeus arrived in a thunderclap, primed for a feud.

You dare attack my home, Sàngó? Sàngó laughed, thrilled,
for Zeus' arrogance would sweeten his vengeance.
Let he without fault throw the first bolt! How d'you feel?

Find yourself ... wanting? Zeus? Thrice you've struck my palace!
/ My aim was not for you! For men! Those bolts I threw
to smite them. / Zeus, killing innocents is callous.

And my palace is wrecked. Redress is what I'm due!
/ And of all the ways, Sàngó, furnishings? You crush
furniture? Are we men or are we Gods? yelled Zeus

Choose better! He turned, snapping his fingers, the lush
beauty returning to the halls as though Sàngó
hadn't happened. Zeus, weakened by the effort, flushed.

Your power dwindles Sàngó said *You've turned yellow.*
Are you well? / Of course! Zeus snapped *Let us settle this*
as Gods. A race! My kingdom to yours. Your might thrown

against mine. The loser answers the victor's whims
for an age, and the victor can take a mortal
from the loser's world. / *Done!* Sàngó hissed, his bolt swift

in his grip. Hera rolled her eyes at how mortal
Gods could be, how like men to reduce disputes down
to sporting feats, but it was done: the stakes, awful,

the route to run, Zeus in his great and golden crown,
in a monstrous gold chariot, Sàngó displeased
on his black bolt, face frowned, awaiting the countdown.

BOOM! They launched off the Plain of Thessaly in Greece,
off the Meteora monasteries. Zeus galloped
into speed, Sàngó's bolt behind, beneath, a crease

in the night skies shedding stormclouds, leaving Europe,
crossing the Mediterranean. Zeus dipped, swerved
into Sàngó's path who to avoid the clash up,

turned sharply and smashed into the Acacus herd
of stout mountains in western Libya. Zeus flashed
forward but Sàngó's anger powered him ahead

over Niger, where Zeus blinded him with a blast
of light and in the chaos cheated, strapped Hermes
– winged Greek messenger God, to his chariot's shaft!

And this was normal. The tax-dodging mortal Greeks
cheated so often they prayed for victory; pleas
so sincere their gods absorbed their dark energies.

Gods exist beyond time and space and all of this
happened lightning-quick, in a mortal's blink. Focus
on Modupe, young, playing in Nigeria ... bliss

one second, mayhem the next, engulfed in monstrous
brutal lightning ... for Zeus chose her as his mortal.
Zeus won that race. Osún feared for Modupe, thus

from a young age trained her to wrestle, would bundle
her chest flat, deepen her voice and send her to bouts
where she battled, bested each man ... until this duel.

It was different. Modupe tried to knock out
Zeus, but he was a God. Much like a match struck in
full sunlight is how mortals look before the clout

of Gods, such is their splendour, and Zeus, transforming
into each beast he'd taken mortals with (a swan
for Leda, a white bull for Europa, even

the Eagle for the child Ganymede) broke the brawn
of Modupe's true grip and bested her. He took
her on the shores of her own river. An aeon

passed in that blink of an eye, for Modupe shook
at each violation, suffered each push, each like
a drill sunk into her womb, shredding, she gushed brooks

of blood, parts of her dissolved, eyes whitened, each spike
of him cut at her spirit. She sobbed for her flesh,
that all she was she could not protect. When she'd strike

at him, Zeus would tighten his nooselike grip afresh.
From the heavens above, Osún saw what Zeus was,
the monster of him turning Modupe to mesh.

She took arms to strike Zeus but Sàngó barred her doors
and spoke the stakes of their race, his face slashed with pain,
anxious, unsure of what attacking Zeus might cause.

Osún railed at him. *This was your fault! You're to blame!*
As they quarrelled, Zeus ... finished. The skies flashed white flames.
He cast Modupe aside, took his chariot's reins

and left the waters still, Modupe deathlike, drained.
Gods exist beyond time and space, and so the child
was born instantly. Demi. That's what he was named.

Half Nigerian mortal. Half Grecian God. Half-child
of Zeus. Half-lord of river waters. He would grow
to possess odd gifts. He had, instinctive and wild

a great sense of height and he could cry river-bowls
of tears. The bastard son of Zeus born by swamp trees:
OluDemi Modupe, Half-God of Rainfall.

Their first months were tough. OluDemi cried small seas
that gushed from his cot and nothing first-time mother,
lone parent, abused girl Modupe did appeased.

Her cries for her body and ill-got child, bothered
nearby rivers to burst their banks and flow inland,
surrounding their home, locking them both in water.

In these churning orbs, it became unclear whose hand
called which waters, to whom which tears belonged; they flowed
into each other ... and began to understand

slowly, that moods rise like tides, that needs change bloodflow.
Like this they bonded. Despite the difficulty
of whence he came, she marvelled to watch Demi grow.

Two things Modupe would never forget. His glee:
when Demi became the Rainman was the second.
The first, the much darker: how Demi was conceived.

ACT

TWO●

BOOK I

When Bolu, King of the Court saw the skill dormant
in the Half-God, he took Demi under his wing
to teach the fine points of basketball. He would rant.

Part in praise of Demi, part critique, part ambling
through battle philosophy, part practical points:
You must be Point Guard. With your small size, your shooting,

you can't really be nothing else so I appoint
you Starting Point Guard. This eagle-eye gift of yours
to see the court from above? You're the starting point!

What do point guards do? / We'll get to that in due course.
First, warfare is based on deception, so attack
when you seem unable to, and when using force

move like you are not. When you are near, you must act
like you're far, and when afar, as if you're near.
To fight and conquer in all your battles shows lack

of supreme excellence. Excellence is to tear
your foe's resistance down without fighting, Demi!
Understand? / No! Bolu owned one book, a dog-eared

copy of *The Art of War*, used it to teach key
aspects of basketball. Unorthodox were his
methods but so potent were the results – army

tactics to treat each teammate as a squad, to seize
and command them thus – that both Gods of War, Ògún
and Ares, would eavesdrop. Demi, our Half-God, breezed

through the lessons. Turned half general, half typhoon,
he would still 'Make it rain' on the court but became
a master tactician. That first year, the platoon

Demi led won most games, the next year were proclaimed
champions. Year after, Demi steered the senior team
to local semi-finals where the Rainman name

drenched every ball court and the spectators would scream
when he touched the ball. After two years, Demi led
the nation's team and his town was a shrine to him:

Rainman banners across each street, small cloud-headed
figurines sold on beaded necklaces, prayers
and libations poured in his name. That name, whispered

in deepest hope by the townsfolk – such areas
of silent meditation are grounds on which Gods
are born. And far above the earth, Sàngó, who stirs

the skies to howl, whose footsteps dictate the roughshod
beat of storms, who regretted his hotheadedness
which had led to Demi's birth, saw further discord.

He gathered the Gods together in the greatness
of heaven's hall and spoke. *The half-boy grows stronger.*
This should stop because smaller gods feel a weakness.

Some prayers due them now feed him and the longer
this persists, we too will grow weak but Elégba,
trickster God and Guardian of Crossroads, spoke softer.

His father is not of this land, we can't ... hamper
him without consent. Then Hermes announced himself.
I am the emissary of Zeus, his father.

As Zeus' godblood pumps through the boy, Zeus himself
weakens. His godpowers draw from Zeus. Zeus demands
action. The boy lives here, the task falls to yourselves.

Zeus says: remember the Agreement? The boy stands
in direct opposition to ...   /   What Agreement?
Sàngó asked. *From all mortal sports, Half-Gods are banned.*

Òrúnmilà, your sage is versed in its contents.
I must leave you now. Hermes strapped fast his sandals.
Their legendary wings flapped and he was gone, absent,

so missed Òrúnmilà recounting the scandal
around the Agreement, hush falling, and his gaze
coming to rest on Sàngó. *It's yours to handle.*

Sàngó, can you cripple the boy? A lightning graze?
Blaze through a leg ...   at which point Osún had enough.
Seriously? His mother Modupe, born here, raised

here, my priestess, is of this land. Demi is of
this land and deserves our protection! Or women
don't matter? Sàngó cleared his throat. *I can blaze off ...*

YOU HAVE DONE ENOUGH! Osún roared. *Useless henchman!*
Doing Zeus' dirty work when you are stronger?
Òrúnmilà spoke: *I see why you hate this plan.*

But something must be done. If Sàngó can't alter
the boy's body then you, Osún, must make him stop.
I cannot, Osún said, *I swore to the far stars*

and beyond, to the Galaxy, yet failed to stop
that defilement. Demi was conceived on my watch.
All that brings them joy is this mortal game, his shot,

that gift, his curse, and you stand here, you Gods who watch
humanity, you Infinites who know how short
each human life is, each sickness-ridden thin notch

on the trunk of eternity, asking I halt
their lone source of joy? / Compassionate as you are,
great Osún, Òrúnmilà said, *Goddess, whose forts*

are streams and healing pools, this must be done, for stars
witnessed the Agreement, all God-Kings gave their word.
Some made personal sacrifices. We risk war.

This is the consequence. Battle. Shield. Spear and sword.
Conflict amongst the Gods. This must be avoided.
Osún sighed so deeply Earth's rivers shrunk inwards.

Well ... give me time. Demi still sleeps in his childbed
by his mother. Yet to reach manhood, the prayers
that feed him are streams compared to our ocean spreads.

/ As you wish, Osún, but he feeds off our prayers,
is of this land, the task is ours, Sàngó owes Zeus.
Fail, and Sàngó's thunderbolts will be your nightmares.

He'll tear chunks from the boy and death might be induced.
GET IT DONE. This meeting is over. The Gods went,
save Sàngó, who knelt by Osún, seeking a truce.

My husband, if you'd listened to me, these events,
none would have come to pass! / I know, Osún, I know.
The fault is mine. What can I do to make amends?

Sàngó's voice shook as he spoke, worries grooved his brow.
If you're sincere, whatever your actions, before
any move, report to me? And Sàngó bowed low.

BOOK II

Though what Zeus did to Modupe desecrated
the sacred swampland on which her compound was made,
and though her son's successes had generated

other houses, Modupe could not sleep or fade
towards slumber anywhere else. She'd always come
back to that first house, the shrine where she'd feel the shade

and shallow shaping of Osún's cool, pull and hum
her to dewy soundless slumber. Metres away
the river would shush itself. The near world would numb

to deepen her sleeping. In this hushed hallowed way
Osún appeared to Modupe in a dream.
They conversed at length, in whispering and wise ways,

Goddess to high-priestess. God-mother to esteemed
God-daughter. Mother to mother. Spirit to child.
Modupe spoke of little happenings that beamed

her back to the attack: a flash of light, a wild
bird above would trigger it and she'd be a scream
beneath Zeus again. His fists. Her throat. She asked why

it happens? Keeps happening? What exact regime
teaches males to take what isn't given? What riles
them? Osún saw Modupe's anger. How it gleamed.

She let it dim, then spoke of the threat to the child –
would Demi stop playing? *I can't ask that of him.*
That ballgame is all he loves! Modupe replied.

I thought as much, Osún said, *but Sàngó has him*
in his sights. Gods have spoken. One who comes against
us does not live long. Osún hummed a quiet hymn,

a water's warmth that calmed Modupe, then grew dense,
tempestuous as monsoon tides, so violent
Modupe cried out. Osún spoke then, her voice tense.

Hush, child. This is what you do. Make him radiant.
Take Demi somewhere else, far from these shores to where
prayers that feed him won't reduce our nourishment.

The task will fall from Sàngó if Demi leaves here.
Go to the Americas where his sport is prime.
If he is skilled enough, his powers will grow there.

He might draw less strength from Zeus, but we haven't time.
There are sports scouts visiting from that foreign land
seeking new talent, I'll bring one by. He must shine.

Demi must 'Make it rain', the scout will watch him pound
that game. Accept any offer that's made and go!
/ It will be done Osún, your seed finds willing ground.

BOOK III

The year is two thousand and nine, the location:
Oracle Arena, four years after he signed
the National Basketball Association's

contract. Game six. Finals. Demi shouts to remind
his team to focus. Fist clenched, arm out, holding court,
his sign to stay in formation as the ball climbs

back up to his open palm. Demi stops just short
of the half court line, shuts his eyes. His consciousness
rises up to the thousands of bulbs buzzing bursts

of light, small suns scorching the players. He watches
the opposing team ready against his, smiles – blink
and it's gone – then he makes his move. Demi rushes

forward, fakes a drive, pivots left so his guard thinks
the ball will come his right as Demi   outlets   to
the power forward, steadfast in his lane, the brink

of the rim a [+] target he knows to ignore, to
swing to the centre, who, though minotaur-like can't
shake his man, and the small forward is waiting to

step up, catch the ball from the chest-pass, throw a scant
fake as he makes for the top of the key,   g l i d   e   it
to the shooting guard to dribble down the line, plant

himself there and taunt the defence till two commit
and Demi, waiting top of the key, like he knew
they would is defence-free, the play-cycle complete,

to receive the ball and pause. Demi looks up, views
the shot clock, the | 00:04 | seconds left locked in its grip
as the world   s l o w s   and Oracle Arena glues

itself to the Half-God, gasps as his fingertip
strokes the blur down, crossover, up, down, crossover,
up and back for the | 00:03 | his elbow pulled back, whip/

/lash wrist-flick the | 00:02 | air trembling the sonarrrrrr
silence of Demi's gift. | 00:01 | Swish. Nothing but net.
| 00:00 | A buzzer-beating last shot. Game over.

Demi's team the Golden State Warriors win. Sweat
clings to his cream skin as a thousand cameras
flash, the Arena rises to its feet, to wet

its twenty thousand lips with Demi's moniker
cascading to him like praise song: *Rainman! Rainman!*
chants rising like incense smoke from sacred altars

or animal sacrifice, burning for Gods and
riding them all: Demi, who had gone from the wee
kid who cried to the boy who came off Nigerian

courts to be reborn, Half-God in 'God's own country'.
God Daymn! Demi whispered, *If anything was meant
to be, it's me. It's this.* Indeed, millions agreed.

Newscasters, journalists, sports companies hellbent
on monetising the myth of him would call him
the sport's prophet, its second coming, heaven-sent.

Reports covered blogs, headlines crossed broadsheets calling
for Demi's induction into the hall of fame
for he broke every three-point record set, scoring

impossible shots. In press conferences, school games,
board meetings, lecture halls, synagogues, in saunas,
cafes, churches, in post offices, Demi's name

ran the full gamut of their lips. Many corners
in many cities echoed their faith in his gift
and accordingly, Demi's powers grew stronger.

His mildest mood swings would cause storm patterns to shift
overhead and darken his world beneath. Mains pipes
would burst, subways flood, all this unconscious, too swift

for him to stop. Three different pairs of eyes had gripes
with this. The first, Modupe, chastised her son:
No excuses, Demi, tune out from all this hype!

Calm down when you're moody! Ah?! Don't blot out the sun!
The second pair of eyes were Hera's – Greek God Queen
who returned to Mount Olympus spinning Zeus yarns.

She exaggerated stories of what she'd seen,
of Demi's powers, his influence on men, how
this sapped Zeus' strength and would completely weaken

him if left to grow unchecked. Zeus nodded and scowled
with Hera, swallowing her stirring viperous
breath. *It will end,* Zeus said. *I know exactly how,*

and low thunders rumbled all round Mount Olympus.
Last pair of eyes arrived with a cough, a polite
request for some of Demi's time. *Yes, please! Of course,*

our Half-God replied and ushered in the slim, light-
footed gentleman. *Sit, Hakeem Olajuwon!*
You are a legend! I cannot believe my sights!

Ha! Here! My boys will die when I tell them. You won
back-to-back championships in nineteen ninety four
and five, the first Nigerian to! Ah! You're a don!

Hakeem 'The Dream' Olajuwon?! Please! Demi poured
gin and cracked two kola nuts, as is tradition,
but saw the small-talk, laughter and pleasantries thaw

as Olajuwon took a large last gulp and shunned
Demi's offer of more. He asked harshly *Parents.*
Who are they? / My parents? That's free information.

Mother's name is Modupe. Father's been absent.
See ... I never knew him. / And are they both mortal?
/ Pardon? / Answer me OluDemi, this instant!

/   *Hakeem, you have overstayed your welcome. The hall ...*
/   *I've watched you play. You're one of us. Our sage, Demi,*
Òrúnmìlà? *My grandfather. There's a roll call*

of Half-Gods. Alonso Mourning comes from Kali,
the Hindu Goddess, destroyer of ignorance.
Iverson, greatest ball handler? Vishnu. Reggie?

Miller? Satet's son – archery Goddess. Leprechauns
made Kevin McHale of the Celtics and Aido-
Hwedo? Rainbow-snake Goddess? Dennis Rodman's aunt.

Clyde Drexler descends from Prometheus, that old
great Greek. Allvis Norse God of wisdom? Jason Kidd's
great-great-grandfather. The years we played were pure gold.

All gone. We had to sign a pact after the kid.
After Jordan.   /   What happened?   /   Jordan, that far-flung
son of Amun-Ra, oldest of Gods, Jordan did

what no one had dared –   flew –   on the court. With no song,
charm or spell to cloak his flight! Live television!
Grandfather had to wipe memories. Everyone's.

Think of the effort it took to weave new visions
for millions of people. To plant them seamlessly.
That brought forth the Agreement: Without exception,

Half-Gods were forbidden from mortal sports and we
agreed to be phased out. We stood by it. Till you.
So Demi, who defies the Agreement? Tell me.

Who is your father? / Zeus / ZEUS? / He beat mother blue.
Pinned her down. Then ... forced his ... the Òrìṣà stood there.
Did nothing. Mother couldn't tell me. How? Could you?

One night, I drank with a loose-lipped mystic who bared
the whole story. I sloshed to Mother's home and asked.
She shrunk before me, into a gnarled root, still scared.

Her hands shook / I was once a vibrant thing. Once fast,
a runner, flashing through the trees. Always wondered
if I should have worn more. Too much flesh in that vast

forest, too much life. My fault? I must have glimmered
like a star to him. The sky turned white. He was there.
He was everywhere. Over, around and under

and inside. I prayed for death. Òrìṣà could hear,
I could feel their presence. They did nothing. At all.
Zeus left. I stood up but their gaze had turned to glares.

I was a blot on their conscience. A stain. A foul
shame. We left, came here. I tried to rebuild my soul,
but these white people, clutching their bags at the mall

when they walk past me. Poor ones calling me a cold
black bitch. I want to say No, cold African bitch
and laugh in all their faces. I have to be cold.

Sometimes I need a wall up. The few I've let hitch
up my skirt since, when we give in to our passions,
when I want them harder, when we lock eyes, I switch

from wading deep in theirs to asking whose actions
are these? Who is looking back? Zeus? Gleaming in them?
Smiling like he did back then? And it just worsens.

Demi, when I feel vengeful, lustful, I feel them.
His eyes. Loving every moment. The sky rumbles
for rain and he is there. Sudden bright lights. Mayhem.

He is there. Headlights, camera flash, I stumble
and he is there. Sudden movements and he is there.
Everywhere. I couldn't keep him out. He crumbled

me down to this. I still can't keep him out. I'm here.
My body is, my body healed, but my mind is ...
I can't control it. What he took from me is clear –

control of my most precious self. But he did this:
he gave me you.   And then she kissed me. My forehead.
You see what was done? The Gods. And she could still kiss.

Still love me. / Terrible thing, Demi, Hakeem said,
But the Agreement you are breaking, who backs you?
To do this on your own is madness. It's unheard.

/ ÒRÌṢÀ OR OLYMPIAN, NO GOD BACKS ME! Fool!
Hear this and ye gods if you're listening, Fuck Zeus,
Sàngó, fuck every ... / Boy, best hold your tongue, be cool.

They're not to be trifled with. Defy them, you'll lose.
One who goes against Gods does not live long and trust,
Zeus is the most vengeful ... / Two years, two, then I use

his own show, the London Olympic Games, to crush
every team. With the world watching this cursed gift will
expand exponentially and there will be gusts

of drowning darkness blowing, climbing over hills,
valleys and cities towards Olympus. The earth
will part, water will walk, I will crest its waves till

Olympus falls and the reckoning of my birth
is answered. I'll defy him utterly! Hakeem,
you are either with me or against, and your worth

to me is that answer; choose wisely. Shame. You seemed
different, but you're just as weak. Show yourself out.
Don't cross me, or I'll make a nightmare of The Dream.

ACT

THREE

BOOK I

Among the Greeks there is a famous tale of pride,
about a child strapped with feathers and wax. It's told
this child who got too close to the sun fell and died.

Whenever and however this story unfolds,
it's never admired that he   flew   that he proved
it was possible, knew it, that – wings – fluttered bold,

bright, b r o a d, a graceful glide of a thing and it moved
towards the horizon before gravity pulled.
His vengeance needed greatness. Demi understood

the need to go further; become legend. It ruled
his waking life, his every dream. His conviction
burned in him ... then burned him out ... to a pitiful

shadow of a man, whisper of a God. A shunned
silence of graveyard-weight and a soup-**thick** darkness
held him. The year: two thousand and twelve. Location:

London, Olympic Stadium, changing room, a mess
of ice packs, drowned towels, frustration and regret.
Hours earlier, first quarter, despite their best

Nigeria trailed America forty-nine nets
to twenty-five. Halfway, seventy-eight points to
forty-five and nothing Demi did worked, from threats

to his team to deep-reading *The Art of War* to
inventing new plays on the spot. Even his shots
fell short   and slow murmurs like low tides began to

rise in the crowd, questioning if the rain had stopped,
asking whether the Rainman's reign had finally
dried up, for captained by Demi, Nigeria lost

by the largest margin in the whole history
of Olympic basketball. The final scores were
one hundred and fifty-six to seventy-three.

Fans were furious. If mid-game you'd scanned them ... there!
Thirty-seventh row, far far right, you might have seen
Hera – Greek God Queen, in human disguise, her hair

twisted in a popular style, skin dimmed to seem
like any mortal but a tide of discontent
spreading from her lips, her influence i n f e c t i n g

the crowd. By her, someone so short he was a dent
in the earth, the unknown God of Gravity, who,
to make amends for the Icarus affair, lent

his service to any deity that asked and through
the match pulled Demi's shots, so each fell short. The Queen
waved to dismiss him. She vanished and appeared through

the steam in the changing room, solidifying
to full Goddess form before a forlorn, naked
Demi. *Demi. Why so sullen? What's wrong? You seem ...*

... broken. You know who I am. Good. What clouds your head?
What is ruffling your nappy feathers? So naive.
That was a scrap of Zeus' power, just a shred.

You've heard that one who goes against us does not live
long? Your days are numbered. But should you go to Zeus,
kneel before him, confess your plot, he will forgive

his son, expand your little powers ... Shhh! Just choose,
and wisely, small god, think, then talk. The door will be
open for two days more. You've time to call a truce.

When Hera left, Demi to dodge journalists, eased
out the back-alley entrance of the stadium
and walked, hood up, through throngs of disappointed kids

asking what had happened to him. Demi sat numb
shrunken down on the bus, a fallen God among
men. He was used to press conferences but these drummed

within him, their questions pitched, rolled and rocked like strong
currents, sloshing from their mouths. He felt himself shrink,
phase in and out, grow weak as though his blood flowed wrong.

Seeking a calm stretch of water, by pure instinct,
the Half-God of Rainfall leapt blindly off the bus
by the River Thames. Its low tide slowed him to think.

All the records I've broken, right from the playoffs,
the most three points last season, ninety-three buckets
in a row in practice, all that ... gone. I'm a curse

to my team, now powerless against Zeus. Fuck it.
Maybe he isn't so bad. I mean ... he ...   Demi,
waiting by traffic lights, hands deep in his pockets,

couldn't complete the thought. It felt like blasphemy.
It repulsed him. Then a large hand clamped his shoulder
and squeezed. Back in America, Modupe reeled.

Her head snapped back. She felt that hand and fell over
by her shrine, calling for Goddess Osún to keep
Demi safe from the coming omens that smouldered

with that large hand, such danger in its calloused grip.
Beneath the traffic lights, Demi winced. *Who are you?*
/ *Elégba, Guardian of Crossroads. You're on my strip.*

/ *An Òrìṣà? What d'you want from me?* / *To show you.*
To show EVERYTHING. And the city of London
blinked out of existence. The entire world blurred blue

and shrunk to the marble earth was from space, and on,
on and on they flew. Before Demi knew it our
solar system was mere memory. His mind turned

somersaults, screaming in him as they passed towers
of comet-clusters, flying till they too were specks
of dust in the distance, dodging solar powder,

cosmic sandstorms, glowing in the many-mooned wreck
of space, past constellations jewelling darkness
till they edged the galaxy and Earth was one fleck

of light. *Can't go further,* Elégba said. *We're blessed*
to have come this far. Easy, Demi. Now look, look.
With Zeus' eyes, look. There, the Sloan Great Wall. Immense.

It's dressed end to end with galaxies, every nook
of it is full ... one point four billion light years
wide ... there are celestials there to whom we are spooks

on a speck .   of a speck .   of a speck .   And we tear
at each other? Squabble for power? We hardly
exist! We're hope. Nothing else. Yet, our deepest fear

is not our insignificance but that we're free,
immeasurable. This is why Zeus comes against you.
Zeus, he is threatened by your possibilities.

Men have faith! In you! All you do ... is shoot.   /   I should
make peace. You think so? asked Demi. *In the grand scheme*
of things, Demi, it does not matter what you do.

Elégba snapped his fingers, Earth returned, sunbeams
restoring warmth to them. *But the choice, how to live,*
is yours. This is Portara Naxos. The sand gleams.

Such a waste of an island. Greeks are ... regressive
sometimes ... who am I to judge? Anyway, that huge
marble doorway? No, over there. It's exclusive.

Entrance to Olympus, home of Greek Gods, refuge
for rare mortals. You're both. Fight Zeus? Make peace? Good luck.
Elégba vanished.   Demi wished for subterfuge,

that surprise would make this go well. *Deep breath* and stuck
one leg s l o w l y through, his whole torso next and there
he was, grand hall, Mount Olympus, the vast white bulk.

He sucked down the urge to run, yelled *Hello? I'm here.*
Hera? Zeus? Father? Column after column stretched
towards the roof, its marble weight wondrous to bear.

Spears, giant shields, monuments of heroes were perched
on marble plinths, bathed in deep shadows. Demi walked
among them, calling *Hello? I don't like to lurch*

in shadows like this. Hello? Zeus, I've come to talk.
I'm your son! Or rather, I'm what you forced into
Mother ... Hello! He slowed by one statue and balked

at how lifelike it looked. Then it moved. Demi flew
back. *You're alive ... Hercules?* / *No. Aaahh ... Move over.*
He is there, half turned to stone. His pulse is ... *faint ... Ouuuh ...*

You ... must ... run, brother. Zeus has gone mad, he glowers
with rage. He did this, took our powers. Perseus
is my name. You're the last free Half-God. Take cover.

Run! Before it's ... It's too late.   With a hideous
crack of thunder, Zeus BOOMED into the hall, almost
returned to his full and supreme strength, tremulous

with unchecked power, he towered over them, thrust
out his arm, grabbed Demi by the neck, plucked him off
the floor. *Now, I'm complete.* Demi squirmed in the roast

of that grip, black neck scorched in that white fist, he coughed
as Zeus squeezed. Zeus placed a flat hand on Demi's chest,
drew out a blue light and, absorbing it, he scoffed

and shimmered marble-white until he grew to crest
the hall's ceiling, crushed Demi's neck completely, cast
the lifeless thing aside and left, laughed as he went.

BOOK II

In the skies above Nigeria, thousands of miles
over seas and deserts, the River Goddess felt
Demi die. The pain was familiar. Sharp. Close. Vile.

She had felt it the day Modupe's mother knelt
on Modupe for the womb sacrifice, felt it
when Zeus violated Modupe, and now smelt

Demi's burned flesh. Osún wailed. She screamed and it split
the silence of the deep, the bones of Gods juddered
in them, the stars dimmed. Sàngó appeared, teeth grit,

for ten thousand rivers loud is her scream, shuddered
before her. *My wife! What is wrong?* / *Zeus has killed him.*
Demi is gone. Now, Thunder-God! Be disorder!

Be chaos! Show what you're made of! Osún, face grim
waved her wrist and Modupe appeared, also
weighted with Demi's death. They collapsed, wrapping limbs

around each other's grief. Sàngó readied his low
bolt, they mounted and were gone, mourning, thundering
to Mount Olympus, storm clouds exploding below,

above and behind them as they passed, retracing
the route back across Niger, through the Acacus
stout mountains, over the Mediterranean

to the Plain of Thessaly, into Olympus.
They found Hera knelt by Demi's side. *Step away!*
yelled Modupe.   *I wanted no fighting! This was ...*

Hera stuttered *This was not my doing. No way
would I condone this.* / *Step back,* Osún said, and knelt
by Demi. She summoned a bathing pool to spray

and do the best she could, embalming him, heartfelt
water-pourings of purest dew, when Zeus stepped in
towering above them. *Now, Sàngó! Make him melt!*

*Battle and crush him, smite him, ensure his feeling
is as mine, his pain as treacherous.* / *I ... cannot,*
said Sàngó, *I'm in his debt. It is forbidden.*

It would start conflict amongst the Gods. I cannot.
/ *But look what he ...* / *I'll fight,* Modupe said, her head
close to Demi's. *You're mortal, you'll die. You're distraught*

but think clearly, Sàngó said. *I'm already dead.*
He was my life. Zeus has killed me again – she stepped
around Demi – *but now, this time, his blood must shed.*

/ *I'll pour myself into you,* Osún said, *I'll help,*
said Hera, *if you let me* / *I too …* a voice said
in the shadows out of which Helen of Troy stepped.

What he did to you he did to my mother … shed
her blood, took her. I will have vengeance. / *As will I* /
I will too! / *He must bleed!* / *Zeus must fall!* They were spread

throughout the hall, hundreds of women, low and high,
in corners, on plinths and grounds below, demigods,
mortals, conceived by women Zeus abused, they cried

I will help too! Zeus just laughed. *THIS IS ALL YOU'VE GOT?*
Sàngó thrust his darkest fire, his closest friend,
his best bolt towards Modupe. *You'll have my blood.*

My every spark. You diminish him. Bring his end.
Quench such arrogance! Zeus wrapped lightning bolts around
each fist like boxing gloves, looked at her and beckoned.

*Bow before me and I'll go easy on you, pound
softer this time.* Modupe crouched down, readied her
self, tasted sweet vengeance and leapt. She left the ground.

When Zeus leapt, these were his gathered powers: Storm Herd.
Marshal of Clouds. Supreme Sky God. God of harvest
and crops. King-God-All-Father. Lightning and Thunder:

ten thousand times stronger than Hera at her best.
When Modupe leapt, these were her powers: Osún –
rivers, Sàngó – thunder, Hera – Greek Queen Goddess

of marriage and birth, Zeus' children – their faiths tuned
to her fists, Yemoja – Òrìṣà deep water
Goddess, the Furies – Greek spirits of vengeance, tuned

their hefty powers too. All would have been slaughtered
by Zeus, save for one thing, Modupe's heart. You need
an atlas to map how vast the heart is, broader

than horizons, deeper than seas, able to feed
off equal parts love and pain, which now tumble through
her veins. She was a reckoning, a dark hybrid.

Some doubt crossed Zeus' mind, and when they met, Zeus knew
and remembered such power. It was a titan's
clash renewed. First punch woke every thunder-god, blew

out their ears. The next one caused floods. Grecian islands
sank and Nigerian cities flooded. Wild cyclones
burst from riverbanks. Stray lightning struck far farmlands.

Olympus itself rocked. Demigods ran as stone
and marble rained. Òrìṣà, Olympians, dumbstruck
by the awesome power on show, together groaned

when Zeus pushed Modupe's head through a plinth. She ducked
out with a sweeping kick that levelled him and brought
Sàngó's bolt down on his chest. Zeus kicked back and plucked

two stone spears, hurling them at Modupe, who caught
one and hurled it back, the other exploding by
her right shoulder. Zeus, already on her, was fraught

with sweat, a lance of lightning in his hands. From high
he called down two thunderbolts, which Modupe blocked
with a shield of hard water, casting waves and tides

at Zeus that slapped him down to stone. Modupe sucked
enough oxygen, launched herself into the sky
cradling a mighty marble orb from the stock

of Olympic sculptures. Zeus aimed a long bow high
to shoot her from the skies, but missed, for precision
wasn't his skill. Modupe struck, and struck him wild

like a comet, cracked the orb across his vision,
again as he fell, harder, each blow: *This is for*
Demi, this, Helen, this, Leda, Danaë, this one

Europa, Antiope ... every mortal who bore
the scar, for the countless, all the women she knew
abused by men, Modupe gathered up their raw

anguish into a primal   *AARGH!*   BANG! She cracked through
his skull. With that last hit, the hall of Olympus
split into pieces like a broken vase and new

wind   blew   through its ancient and hallowed emptiness
now exposed to the world. Rarely does a God's life
flash before its eyes. Zeus saw his. The complete mess.

From the fall of his father by his hand, the strife
of titans, this battle, Modupe's fists, to hell
where Hades, God of the Underworld, his long-life

banished brother, rubbed his palms and whispered *Well, well
brother* ... with a glint in his eyes. And his whisper
was a roar, and all the fires and flames of hell

roared too in perfect harmony. Zeus, so scared for
his soul, he grasped what strength he had left and dashed back
to his flesh. But like a thief who rams a shoulder

at a door to find its wood reinforced, well stacked,
so did Zeus slam back into his body to find
Modupe's dark foot on his pale neck. He went slack.

His lungs slumped. His eyes flashed then dimmed again, his mind
roared and hushed again. The whole sky gasped but stayed still.
Modupe stared deep into his face, hers refined,

her brown eyes black, her anger bitter, her gaze steel,
her rage justified.　　　　Silence swallowed Olympus.
None stirred as Zeus choked beneath her black foot, her heel

grinding his white throat. Then came a legend who thrust
himself at her feet. *Modupe,* prayed Hercules,
I come to you neither hero nor Half-God, just

as a child, his son, asking you spare his life, please.
You are victorious. Olympus is humbled.
Much has Zeus learnt today, he won't forget with ease.

I'll make sure of this. Please let him live. He grovelled
by her feet. Modupe turned to the Goddesses,
all mighty, all silent, not one moved a muscle.

Such was the request. She looked to the pained masses
gathered who had survived Zeus but still wore the scars,
still carried the invisible wounds, and flashes

of rage slashed their mouths. *No. Zeus who is old as stars*
thinks Earth spins for him, that he is entitled to
our bodies. He will never learn. Vengeance is ours.

You must kill him and kill him now. Modupe took
her gaze to Hera, Queen Goddess, Zeus' own wife
who seeing their lucid truth, shaped her hands like so.

Modupe did what she'd planned to. She took his life.
She knelt on, crushing his broken neck, she chased what
light glowed in him, to darkness, to the afterlife.

BOOK III

The year is two thousand and thirteen. Zeus' death
left a ruler's vacuum other thunder gods rushed
to fill but Sàngó, still wracked with guilt, claimed the breadth

of work fell to him. The skies over Greece could rush
and roar if he so pleased but Sàngó sought to fuse
the Gods, a cross-pantheon regime, built on trust.

Osún challenged all the Òrìṣà who, subdued
by her passion, agreed to repercussions, tough
ones too, for mortals and Gods whoever abused.

The mothers and daughters, fathers and sons shared rough
stories of their attacks. The guilty who were free
woke up to crowds chanting *Enough! Enough! Enough!*

Modupe returned all powers when the body
of Zeus was burned, but strands of god-mightiness clung
like mist around her, like rebel-song melodies.

She walked from her shrine to the river's edge where songs
that left her body, turned near waters to healing
pools, and women came to bathe in them, old and young,

from across the world. Modupe's battle-scars gleamed
in the night. Those who dared to ask how she was maimed
would be told in whispers how once she killed a king.

She joined Bolu in coaching basketball, he'd rain
The Art of War at the girls and boys. When Modupe is asked
how best to win a game, she says *Play with love. Play with pain.*